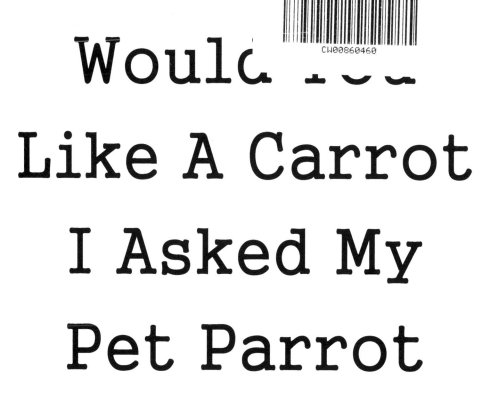

# Would You Like A Carrot I Asked My Pet Parrot

## Words and pictures by Aimee Hughes

Copyright © 2018 Aimee Hughes

"Would you like a carrot?" I asked my pet parrot.

She replied, "No carrot, no crackers, to tell the truth, I am not much of a snacker."

Then
I realized
I left
the monkey
in the kitchen
at dawn.

Now
the bananas
all will
be gone.

I need
to go
and check on
the hippo
in the tub.

He is
probably waiting
for me
to feed him
his grub.

The spider
in the corner
who made a web
so pretty,

finds bugs
on his own,
so he is not
meowing at me
like my
five little
kitties.

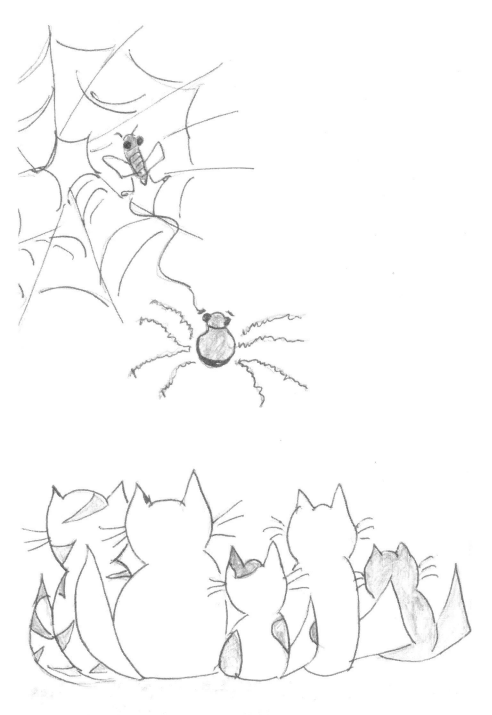

The kangaroo
who is hanging out
on
my couch,

I stuffed
some treats
to nibble,
down
in her pouch.

Do you
think the giraffe
in the closet
is doing okay?

He had
to duck
his head
to go in,
I moved
the coats
out of
his way.

The squirrels
in the attic
provided
their own nuts
to eat.

I suggested
they dip them
in chocolate
to make them
more sweet.

They said
they liked them
to be
served plain.

The raccoons
found the
idea yummy,
but since
getting free food,
they did not
complain.

The dog
wants his
Kibble and Bits
or
a bone.

I told him
he would have
to wait a moment.
I am
really busy
as I am
all alone.

I really
could use
an extra pair
of hands
to
help out.

Maybe
a pet octopus
would be nice,
he has eight,
he would
lend me
a few
no doubt.

The only
problem is
the apartment
is small,
there is
no more space.

Plus
feeding
all these pets
is expensive,
puts a
frown on
my face.

If I had all the money
in the world to buy food,

I would not
turn anyone away.
I would not
have to be rude.

But since
I cannot afford
one more mouth
to feed now,

I will have to
close my doors,
not let in
one single cow.

I ask⋯
do you have
extra room
at your house?

If so,
watch out,
I may
send you
my little
pet mouse!

the end

Other Aimee Hughes books available at amazon and barnesandnoble.com

The Knock—Out King

Dean and the Dinosaur Hunt Mikey's Boxing Gloves

We Were Sitting At A Red Light In An Old Beat—Up Bronco

Eek

The Fluttering Butterfly and the Buzzing Bee series

"Duck" Says Quack

A Mouse Is In Your Trunk

Are You Are Wrinkly Prune With Purple Lips?!

Did You Ever Listen To the Noises Your House Makes?

Humphrey Hippo Has Hiccups

Honk

A Pig On the Pot


And many others…

Printed in Great Britain
by Amazon